P9-BYG-185

Kitty Cat, Kitty Cat, Are You Going To School?

BY Bill Martin Jr and Michael Sampson
ILLUSTRATED BY Laura J. Bryant

two lions

Amazon Publishing
Attn: Amazon Children's Publishing
P.O. Box 400818
Las Vegas, NV 89140
www.amazon.com/amazonchildrenspublishing

Library of Congress Cataloging-in-Publication Data
ISBN-13: 9781477817223 (hardcover)
ISBN-10: 1477817220 (hardcover)
ISBN-13: 9781477867228 (eBook)
ISBN-10: 1477867228 (eBook)

The illustrations are rendered in watercolor paints
and colored pencils on Strathmore paper.
Book design by Vera Soki
Editor: Margery Cuyler

Printed in China (R)
First edition
10 9 8 7 6 5 4 3 2

To my grandson, Rhett Sampson
—M.S.

To my brother Tom and his wonderful family
—L.J.B.

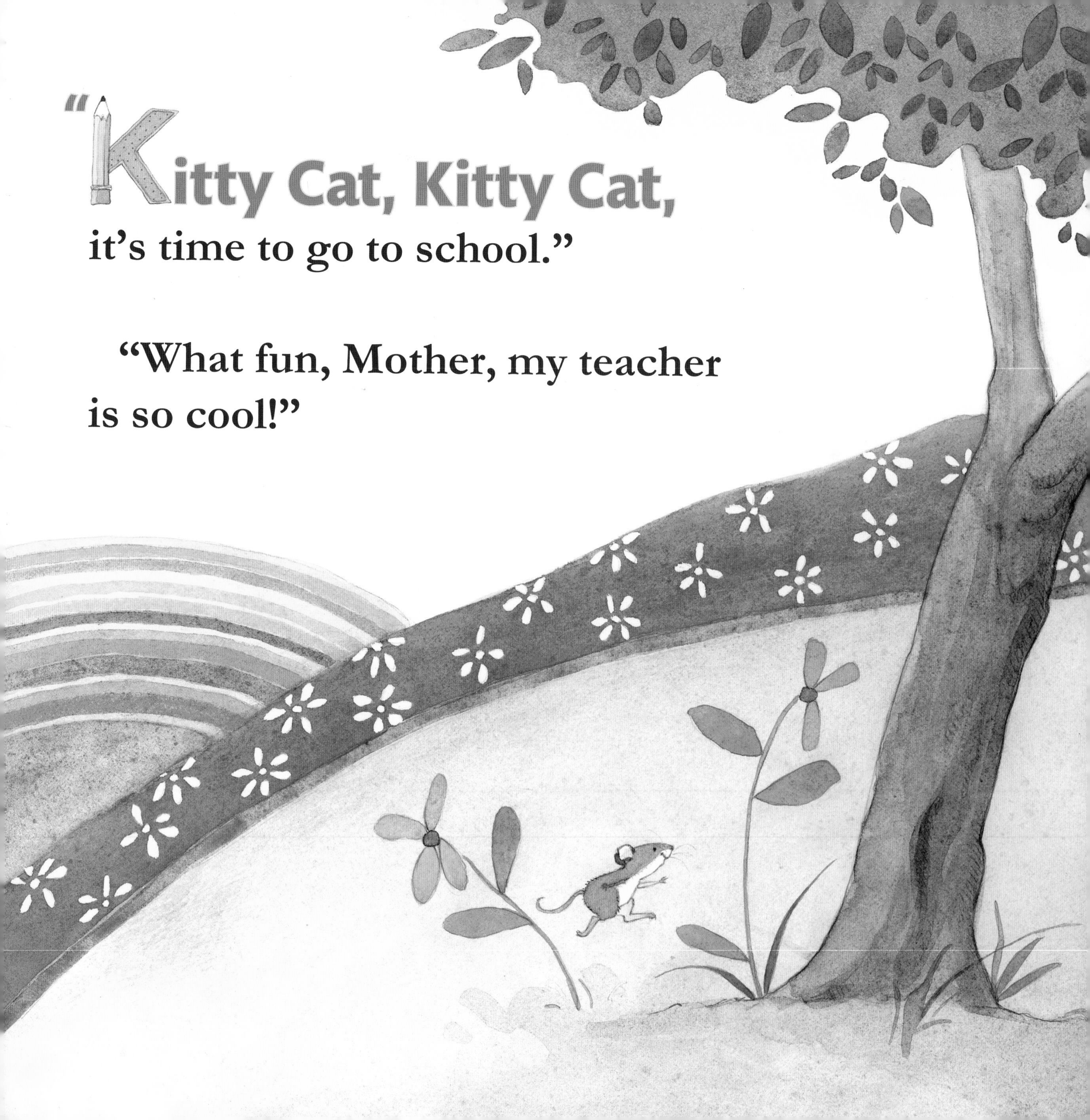

"Kitty Cat, Kitty Cat,
it's time to go to school."

"What fun, Mother, my teacher is so cool!"

"Kitty Cat, Kitty Cat, come sing a little song."

"Okay, Teacher, I like to sing along."

"Kitty Cat, Kitty Cat,
let's open up this book."

"What fun, Teacher. I
see a monkey, look!"

"Kitty Cat, Kitty Cat, can you count to ten?"

"Oh, yes, Teacher, and back to one again."

“Kitty Cat, Kitty Cat,
go outside and play.”

“Yippee, Teacher, my
favorite time of day.”

"Kitty Cat, Kitty cat,
time to have a treat."

"Yum yum, Teacher,
I always like to eat."

"Kitty Cat, Kitty Cat,
you need to take a nap."

"Oh, yawn, Teacher, I'll
curl up in your lap."

"Kitty Cat, Kitty Cat, what's your show-and-tell?"

"Look, look, Teacher, I brought a little bell."

"Kitty Cat, Kitty Cat,
now it's time for art."

"That's great, Teacher,
I think I'll paint a heart!"

“Kitty Cat, Kitty Cat, your day at school is done.”

“Yes, yes, Teacher, and I had SO MUCH FUN!”

1 2 3